Series 497

The Wise Robin

by NOEL BARR

with illustrations by P. B. HICKLING

Publishers: Ladybird Books Ltd . Loughborough
© Ladybird Books Ltd (formerly Wills & Hepworth Ltd) 1950
Printed in England

THE WISE ROBIN

It was cold, very cold; snow lay on the ground, and icicles hung from the roof edge. Ponds were frozen, and children ran about with rosy faces and pink noses. Mr. and Mrs. Robin stayed all day long in the corner of the barn, only venturing out when they were hungry. Food was very difficult to find; the insects which the robins liked were all hidden away in cracks and crevices, not even a spider showed itself.

7214 0199 6

There was one place, however, in which they knew they were likely to find something to eat. This was on the nursery window-sill at the big house. The children put out crumbs two or three times a day; it was a good thing for the robins that they did, otherwise they would have fared badly.

One day, when it felt colder than ever, the robins alighted on the window-sill.

"Dear me," Mrs. Robin said after a while, "these cake crumbs are better than ever to-day, and the currants are delicious!" "I'm glad you like them, my dear," Mr. Robin said between his pecks, "I like these crisp bread crumbs much better." "Bob," said Mrs. Robin, after another pause, "what is that inside the room?"

Bob picked up a large crumb, and hopping closer to the window, looked into the room beyond. On the far side of it there was a Christmas tree. Almost as high as the ceiling it stood, green and branching, a pretty sight. Coloured balls of shining glass hung from it, with gay crackers, bags of sweets, tiny dolls, and all kinds of little animals. Candles, as yet unlit, were everywhere, and from each branch dripped long strands of sparkling silver tinsel.

Both birds stared at the tree for some time, and then Mrs. Robin spoke. " I do like all that silvery moss, don't you, Bob? " she said. But before Mr. Robin could answer, a maid came to the window to shake her duster, and the robins, startled, flew back to the barn.

During the cold weather quite a number of little birds gathered in the barn before nightfall. They slipped in through a broken window, and a badly-fitting door. Such a chattering and a twittering went on, as they told one another their adventures of the day. The sparrows were the noisiest, and the starlings were almost as bad.

"You are very quiet, my dear," Bob said that evening, as he and his wife sat close together. "Is anything the matter?" Mrs. Robin looked up at her husband, then she looked down, and sighed.

"Bob," said she, "I want some of that silver moss for my nest in the spring. Just think how beautiful it would look woven in here and there! How everyone would admire it!"

"No, no, my dear, it wouldn't do at all," Bob said quickly. "Why, it might make our nest shine so much that children would see it, and steal our eggs!"

"Oh no, it wouldn't, Bob," Mrs. Robin said, her bright eyes looking anxiously at her husband, "they would only think it was dewdrops shining in the sun. Oh Bob, *will* you get a little for me? You are such a brave bird, I'm much too frightened to get it myself!"

Mr. Robin was just going to answer his wife when the barn door opened with a squeak and a groan, and all the birds were silent. A man came in, carrying a lantern, which lit up the place with a rosy glow.

He filled a bowl at the corn bin, and then went out again, leaving the barn in darkness as before.

"Bob," said Mrs. Robin softly. "Bob, will you?" Bob looked at his little wife. He liked her to think him brave, and he liked her to have what she wanted, but he didn't like the thought of venturing into the nursery himself. "My dear," he said, "you will soon forget all about it. Shall we talk of something else?"

"Oh dear," Mrs. Robin said in a very tiny voice, "I did think . . . " and a tear rolled slowly down her beak. Then she shook her wings, and said, "All right, dear, I'll try not to think about it . . . " but, unfortunately, after making such a brave speech, she finished up with a loud sob.

Bob turned to her at once. "Don't cry, my dear," he said kindly. "Of course I'll get some for you, I'll get it first thing to-morrow." And soon both little birds put their heads under their wings and went to sleep.

On the following morning, however, it was snowing so hard, and the wind was so strong, that it was really not safe for any small bird to be out. The robins sat in their corner, now talking, now sleeping, and all the time getting hungrier and hungrier. Late in the afternoon, the snow stopped and the sun shone, the children then came tumbling out of the house and were soon busy making a snowman.

The gardener took his broom, and began to sweep the snow from the paths, and the robins flew together to a tree overlooking the nursery window. Bob's eyes brightened when he saw that the snow had been cleared from the sill, which was strewn with crumbs.

"Come along," he said gaily. "Food always makes one feel braver."

They began to eat the crumbs, and
Mrs. Robin was so busy trying to peep at
the silver moss, that she had no idea that
she was eating bread instead of cake.

"Now," said Mr. Robin, when all the
crumbs had disappeared, "if you will go
and wait in the holly bush, my dear, I'll
see what I can do for you," and he puffed
out his red breast importantly.

Bob looked at the window, it was open
a tiny bit at the top, and he saw that the
room was empty. He flew up and through
the window, alighting on the top of a low
cupboard.

Turning his head to look at the Christmas tree, he was almost startled out of his wits! Close to him was a great open mouth, with enormous teeth, and two eyes glared at him fiercely. Bob thought some awful creature was ready to eat him up, he didn't know it was only a rocking horse.

He flew in a great fright to a chair on the other side of the room, but scarcely had he reached it when he was off again, this time to the top of the window curtains, where he sat trembling. Sitting on the chair was a large doll. She had fair hair and big blue eyes, and those eyes had been looking straight at Bob. And now, as he looked round the room, he saw other eyes watching him. On the floor lay a teddy bear staring up at him severely, and in the corner a wooden soldier stood pointing his gun at him.

"Bless me!" Mr. Robin said to himself. "What am I to do?" He looked down into the room again, and then he understood— they were only toys after all, and no more alive than were the tiny ones on the Christmas tree. He sighed a great sigh of relief, then flew down, and sitting on the doll's chair, he pulled her hair. Next he pecked the teddy bear's nose, but he left the rocking horse alone, and went off to the Christmas tree.

The tinsel shone, and the glass balls twinkled in the firelight, and the tiny toys looked at him with tiny eyes.

Bob was very busy trying to find the best and shiniest piece of tinsel for his wife, when he almost jumped out of his skin! The door opened suddenly, and children and grown-ups crowded into the room. The window was closed, the curtains were drawn, and the children skipped and jumped round the tree, telling one another how lovely it was, and clamouring for the candles to be lighted. Bob was too terrified to move.

He cowered there against the slim trunk of the tree, gazing dumbly through the branches at the people round him, hoping and hoping that he wouldn't be seen. And then he felt more scared than ever, for a tall man began to light the candles. The children laughed and chattered, but Bob crouched lower and lower, wondering how soon his feathers would be singed.

Soon the children danced round the tree, singing as they went, and then the tall man called out, "Now for the presents!" The first little girl chose a blue and green rubber ball, and a little boy chose an engine. The third, a very tiny girl, asked shyly for the fairy doll at the top of the tree, and the tall man stood on a chair to reach it down for her.

And then Bob heard the next child say, "Please may I have the toy robin?" And his little heart nearly stopped beating.

"Toy robin?" asked the tall man, "but I don't think there is one on the tree!"

"Yes there is," said the child in a surprised voice — "Look!" and then she pointed her finger straight at Bob, and everyone looked up at him. "So there is," the tall man said, "I wonder how it got there?" And he went round to the other side of the tree to get the chair to stand on.

Bob shook so much with fright that he thought he would fall off the tree. If he didn't do something quickly he would be kept here as a toy robin — in this nursery with the staring doll and the dreadful horse. What could he do? His head was in a whirl . . .

And then suddenly, he knew. The very wisest thing he could do was to show all these people that he was a real, live robin, and not a silly toy.

He stopped trembling, and with fluttering wings he sprang to the topmost branch of the tree. There he threw back his head, opened his little beak, and sang and sang at the top of his voice. His throat quivered, and his breast glowed as red as the holly berries decorating the room. "Oh!" cried the children, and "Oh!" cried the grown-ups, "he's a real one after all, how lovely."

All eyes were on Mr. Robin as he trilled and whistled and chirruped. When at last he stopped, everyone clapped, and the tall man drew back the curtains and opened the window.

"Thank you, little robin," he said, "for making this the best Christmas tree we have ever had. Now fly away home!"

"Goodbye, goodbye, little robin!" called the children, waving to Bob as he flew out into the cold, frosty air. He was so glad to be free that he never once thought of the tinsel.

It was not quite dark, and Bob flew straight to the holly bush. There he found his wife in a terribly anxious state, and so glad to see him that she cared not a bit about the tinsel. They flew back together to the barn, and there she listened open-beaked to the tale of his adventures.

Two or three weeks later when the snow had gone and the sky was blue, and food was plentiful again, Bob found the discarded Christmas tree in the garden.

A few strands of tinsel still hung from it, and when the gardener's back was turned Bob pounced on them eagerly, and took them home to his wife. Mrs. Robin was delighted, and hid them away, and in the spring, when her nest was finished, it was admired by all who saw it.

Series 497